THE DREAM FACTORY

written and illustrated by Nurit Karlin

J. B. Lippincott New York

JE
copy 1

Library of Congress Cataloging-in-Publication Data
Karlin, Nurit.
    The dream factory.

    Summary: A little sheep who doesn't like to go to
bed at night changes her mind after a visit to the
Dream Factory.
    [1. Dreams—Fiction. 2. Sleep—Fiction. 3. Sheep—
Fiction] 1. Title.
PZ7.K1424Dr 1988   [E]   87-45311
ISBN 0-397-32211-9
ISBN 0-397-32212-7 (lib. bdg.)

for
Rama

Baa Baa loves to play all day.

She doesn't like to go to sleep.

But tonight is different.

Grandma is taking her to visit ...

the Dream Factory.

The ride is long, but Baa Baa loves it.

The night is quiet and beautiful.

At last Grandma slows down.

"We're almost there," she says.

One last jump and they're at the door.

Baa Baa rings the bell. "Come in," says the sheep.

"Welcome...

to the Dream Factory!"

Everybody wants to meet Baa Baa.

They show her

how the dreams are made.

Baa Baa plays with the dreams.

"They're all wonderful!" she says.

"We'll send you one every night," the sheep promise.

"And this is a present to take with you now."

"Good-bye," calls Baa Baa. "And thank you!"

Grandma takes the short way home.

"We're almost there," she says, but Baa Baa doesn't hear.

Grandma smiles.

Now Baa Baa loves to play all day.

She also likes to close her eyes…and go to sleep…

and have
another dream.